Ultim Takeover

Alex Lane
Illustrated by Bede Rogerson,
Paul McCaffrey and Kel Dyson

OXFORD

The House

By Alex Lane
Illustrated by Bede Rogerson

Jack stared at the house. The house stared back. Or, at least, that's what he had convinced himself it was doing. In the sky above, metallic grey clouds rumbled, threatening a downpour. Jack shivered in the cool air as he looked at their new home.

Slates hung, slipped and slanted, leaving a hole in the roof and exposing skeletal beams of wood. The guttering had come away and was bent at an awkward angle away from the top of the building. Dark green ivy snaked up the sides of the walls and clung tenaciously to the crumbling brickwork. Jack squinted at the windows on the ground floor, trying to see inside, but they were covered in so much dirt that it was impossible to see into any of the rooms from where he was standing.

He felt his father's hand on his shoulder.

"So, what do you think?" asked his father.

Jack gave a non-committal shrug.

"Come on, son," said his father. "It'll be great!"

It was a phrase his father had been using a lot recently.

Behind him, the car door slammed.

"Is that it?" snorted Stacy, as she pulled one of the earphones out that attached her to her MP3 player.

Jack's sister, Stacy, was fifteen, three years older than Jack. A fact which, she thought, gave her the automatic right to boss Jack around.

It's all right for her, Jack thought, bitterly.

Stacy could still get the bus to her old school and would still see all her friends. But Jack had to move schools. For him everything had changed.

"It just needs a bit of work," said their father.

"It needs pulling down!" complained Stacy.

"It was a bargain."

"Dad," she said flatly, as if he were the child and not her. "You were ripped off."

When their mum was alive Stacy would never have answered back like that, but now … it was as if their dad had lost his fight. Stacy, on the other hand, was up for fighting anything.

"What are you staring at, stupid?" she snapped, glaring at Jack.

Jack turned his head away and looked again at the house. A flagstone path curled round the front, like a lop-sided, toothy grin. Most of the concrete was cracked or covered in weeds and moss, giving it a decayed look. He watched his dad walk towards the front door, fiddling with the tag on the new set of keys. Then he went to the back of the car and opened the boot. It was rammed with Stacy's things, and he had to pull out a black bin liner of her clothes before he could even see his bag. The rest of their stuff would be arriving the following day on a removal truck.

Stacy walked over and pushed Jack to one side. "Move it," she growled.

"Why should I?" he said, coldly.

"Because ..."

"Kids!" shouted their father, who had just managed to open the front door. "Come and look. It'll be ..."

"Great," Jack and Stacy both chimed.

With his bag slung over his shoulder, Jack walked towards the house, kicking at the stinging nettles that lined his route. Even so, he managed to get stung twice before he got to the front door. He took a deep breath and stepped over the doorstep.

The hall was lit by a single light bulb that hung from a cable in the middle of the ceiling. Light struggled to get in through the dirty windows, but the hall was still dark and dingy, and eerie shadows jutted out from each corner. A worn out red carpet wound up a flight of stairs and wooden panels lined the walls.

At the side of the stairs Jack noticed a door. As he stared at it, he swore he saw the handle move. An icy chill ran up his spine.

"Don't think you're going to get the biggest room." Stacy barged past, dragging the bin liner behind her.

Jack was knocked to one side, and he had to grab on to the wooden banister to stop himself falling. "Ow!" he yelled, as a splinter dug into the palm of his hand.

"Hey!" called their dad, from the kitchen. "Be nice!"

"Yeah, right," muttered Jack. He sucked his hand. The splinter was large, so he managed to get it out with his teeth. He spat the wood on to the floor. The splinter had gone in deep. A drop of blood fell on the carpet mingling with the red threads.

That evening, Jack, Stacy and their dad sat round the kitchen table in semi-darkness. All the lights had blown. It was too dark to fiddle around with the fuse box, so they ate their chip supper by torchlight. Behind them, the boiler thumped like a metallic heartbeat. The pipes grumbled and gurgled in the background but the radiators had not come on.

"It's cold," moaned Stacy.

"Sorry, love," said their dad. "I'll try and bleed the radiators tomorrow."

At the mention of bleeding, Jack unconsciously touched the point on his hand where the splinter had gone in.

When they had finished eating, they had a quick game of cards. But with his belly full, Jack began to feel his eyelids grow heavy.

"I think we should all get an early night don't you?" said his dad.

He handed them each a torch and Jack made his way up the creaking stairs. He was so tired, that he hardly noticed the shadows stretching towards him.

That night, Jack twisted and turned in his sleeping bag. He dreamt that he was running through the house, trying to get out, but all the doors were locked. The only one that was open was the one underneath the stairs, the one leading to the cellar. Hot, stale air exuded from the blackness within. Jack took a step towards it. He reached out towards the handle …

Jack woke up exhausted and drenched in sweat. His whole body ached. The thin air bed that his dad had put on the floor for him had deflated during the night, and he could feel the hard wooden floor beneath him. He was still tired, but he knew he would not sleep any more so climbed out of his sleeping bag. It was light outside, but the house did not seem to want to let any of it in. It was permanently gloomy.

He went to the bathroom. His dad had removed the rat with a shovel he had found in the garden and had put it in the dustbin outside. The tap choked out some dirty water. Jack let it run for a while, but it did not clear much. Instead, he decided to clean his teeth using some of the bottled water that his dad had bought.

At the bottom of the stairs, Jack tripped. The pins holding the carpet on the bottom step had come away and the carpet curled upwards. Jack went flying, landing face down. The floorboards moaned as he hit them.

Jack could feel a lump forming above his eyebrow even before he got up. Slowly he got to his feet, feeling a little dizzy and went to examine the step. He was sure the carpet had not been like that yesterday.

In the kitchen, Jack found a note from his dad, saying that he had gone into town. He was going to call into the hardware shop, where he was going to be taking over as manager, and would pick up some fuses. The note also said that he would try to be back for when the removal men arrived.

Jack wet a cloth and put it on his eye just as Stacy came into the room. She was wearing her pink fluffy dressing-gown and slippers.

"What happened to you?" she asked.

"Fell," he replied, grumpily.

"Idiot!"

"Shut up," he snapped.

"Here, let me have a look." She reached up towards Jack's face. He flinched, but he let her remove the cloth. "You'll have a nasty bruise, but you'll be OK."

"Thanks, doctor," he said, sarcastically.

Stacy paused, then said, "Sleep well?"

"No. You?"

"All right," she said, although the bags under her eyes told a different story.

Jack suddenly felt trapped in the house. He needed some fresh air. "I'm going out."

"Where?"

"For a walk."

Stacy bit her lip. For a moment, she looked as if she was going to ask to go with him, but she didn't. "Don't go far then," she said instead.

Jack went to the front door and tried to open it. The handle was stiff, but it finally gave and Jack ran outside.

He didn't stop running until he was round the corner at the end of the road. Then he slowed to a walk. He found a stone and kicked it along the pavement.

I hate that house, he thought. *I hate it. I hate it. I hate it!*

After a minute, he had the sensation that someone was watching him.

It was the girl who had been staring over the fence the previous evening. She was sitting on a swing in the park, alone. They locked eyes, and so Jack crossed the street.

"Hi," he said.

The girl looked at him with curiosity but didn't say anything.

Jack tipped the pool of water off the swing next to her and wiped it dry, then he sat down. "I saw you last night," he persisted, "over the fence."

"Nobody's lived there for years," she said, nodding towards the house.

"Why not?"

"Years and years."

"It was a bargain."

"The last family that lived there disappeared."

"Disappeared?"

"Vanished."

"Sounds like rubbish."

"Maybe," said the girl, pushing off the ground and swinging forwards. "But nobody's been there since."

Jack stared at the back of the gloomy building and shivered.

Jack got back to the house an hour later.

"Hello?" he called out. "Dad?"

There was no answer.

"Stacy?"

Nothing. Jack remembered the girl's words. *Disappeared. Vanished.*

He jumped as he heard a door slam.

"Stacy?" he called again. He ran up stairs, heart thumping, and banged on her door.

"Stacy?" he called. "You in there?"

When there was no answer, he opened the door and went inside. Her stuff had been tipped out of the bin liner and was strewn all over the floor but there was no one there.

Disappeared. Vanished.

The door slammed shut behind him. "Just the wind," he said, more to calm himself down than anything.

He walked over and shut the window and went back downstairs. In the kitchen he found a second note, this time from his sister.

Gone to stay at
Kim's. Will call later.
Stacy x

It was just then that he heard something else … his name being whispered.

Jack.

It was so quiet at first that he did not know if he was just imagining it. But then he heard it again. He walked into the hall and noticed that the door under the stairs was ajar. Hot, stale air exude from the blackness within. The boiler in the kitchen was thumping rhythmically now.

Jack's breathing began to quicken and the hairs on the back of his neck stood up as he went down the stairs. He had the uncomfortable feeling that he was being watched again. This time by the house. It felt as though the house was alive.

Jack felt dizzy as he took a step towards the cellar door. He reached out towards the handle and … and then someone banged on the front door.

The removal men had arrived.

Jack felt better with people around. The house itself had fallen silent, suppressed by all the noise. Jack tried to bury the feeling that the house was just waiting for them to go.

His dad turned up just as the removal men were unloading the last of the boxes from the lorry. They had piled everything in the hall, refusing to carry anything upstairs. Jack's dad had a half-hearted argument with them. But they said that it was not in their contract. He offered to pay them more money but they said that they had another job to go to. Jack watched them climb back into the cab of the lorry. He found himself wishing they would stay.

Together, Jack and his dad spent the rest of

the afternoon shifting boxes around but not really making a serious attempt at unpacking. His dad joked about them having 'dad and lad' time together, but it didn't make Jack feel any better. His mood only began to lift when his dad said he would take him out for tea.

They found a quiet Italian café in town and both ordered large pizzas. His dad chatted about Jack's new school and how nice the teachers had been when he had met them.

"Isn't this great?" his dad said, when they were half-way through their pizzas.

There's that word again, thought Jack. *Great.*

Although Jack felt calmer away from the house, he wanted to tell his dad how much he hated it there, and how he wanted to go back to their old home.

"This is the new start we all needed," his dad said.

It was dark when they left the café. It had begun to rain. As they made their way back to the house in the car, Jack felt his mood sink again. By the time they got home, the wind had picked up.

Jack's dad unlocked the door and flicked on the light. He had managed to change the fuses so the lights worked but the radiators were still not on. Nevertheless it was a lot warmer in the house now. Jack could smell the same stale smell he had noticed coming from the cellar. His dad noticed it too.

"It smells funny in here," he said.

"It's coming from the cellar," replied Jack, holding his nose. "It smells like something's died."

"Maybe there's another rat. I'll check it out in the morning."

Just then, his dad's mobile began to ring. It was the police. The storm had set the alarm off at the hardware shop and he had to go and sort it out.

"Can I come with you?" said Jack.

His dad checked his watch.

"Sorry, son. It's getting late. I don't know how long I'm going to be." He thought about going to get Stacy but by the time he had done that, he reasoned that he could be back from the shop already. So he sent Jack to bed and assured him that he would be as quick as possible.

Jack didn't bother to clean his teeth or get undressed. He just slipped into his sleeping bag fully clothed. The air bed was still down, and so he sat on the hard wooden floor, leaning against the wall. He had not unpacked properly and had only opened a couple of boxes. He pulled out a book from one box. It was a horror story about a boy who found a book. As soon as the boy had read the book he realized it was cursed and bad things began to happen to him.

Jack was halfway through the second chapter in his book, when the bulb in his room blew. He caught his breath and scrabbled around the floor in search of his torch. He pushed the plastic switch and the beam flicked on.

Outside the rain had become a full storm. He could hear the wind howling in the tree outside, as one of the branches began to scratch on the window, clawing at the glass. The house began to groan.

Downstairs, he heard a door creak open.

"Dad?" he tried to call out. But his mouth was dry and the word stuck in his throat.

Jack.

It was as if the sound had just appeared in his head. But then he heard it again more clearly, just like the first time.

Jack.

"Who is it?" he demanded, but he did not have any strength in his voice.

He slipped out of his sleeping bag and opened the door to his room. Jack shone the torch round. The boxes piled in the hall created toothy shadows up the wall.

Jack.

There was a light on downstairs. The walls felt like they were closing in on him. He had to get out of the house. He began to run down the corridor. He got to the top of the stairs. The door to the cellar was wide open now and a hot stinking breath of air wafted up. He knew now it was the house calling him.

Jack.

He heard a ripping noise. The carpet on the stairs was beginning to peel up like a huge tongue. Jack began to run.

Jack.

He had to get out. He had to get out. He jumped, leaping over the last few steps. The carpet licked upwards towards him. He was nearly at the front door. He reached out to the handle and twisted and …

Jack.

Ultimate Takeover

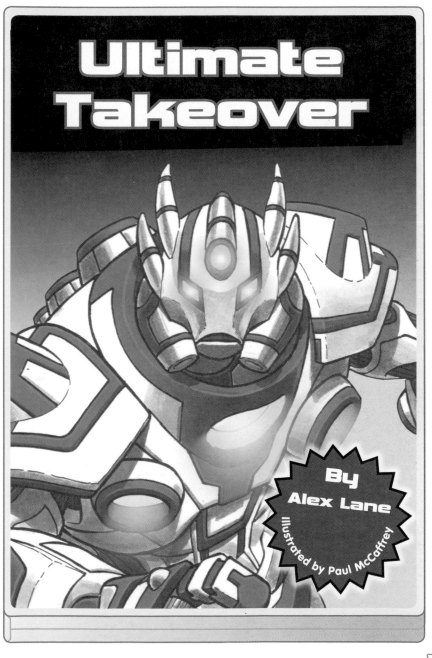

By
Alex Lane

Illustrated by Paul McCaffrey

39

Understanding Film Scripts

Note for the reader:

At the start of each new scene, you will see a heading which tells you where and when it is taking place, e.g. `INT.BEDROOM.DAY`. This tells you that the scene is going to be in an interior setting (inside), in a bedroom, and it is daytime. Where you see `EXT.` this means that the scene is going to be set in an exterior setting (outside).

Each new character we meet is introduced in capital letters to make their entrance stand out, e.g. `Off screen we hear William's MUM shout.`

All dialogue is set in the centre of the page so you can tell it apart from the directions. The name of the character speaking is written above their dialogue.

Where it says `(cont.)` it means 'continued'. It means that the person who was just speaking continues to speak (following an action or a break in the page).

STUDS

A Short Film
by Alex Lane
Illustrated by Kel Dyson

Studs

INT. BEDROOM. DAY.

WILLIAM SPARKS, 11, is lying in bed. He
is staring up at the poster on the wall
above him. The poster is a black and white
picture of the footballer Dixie Dean. Next
to the bed is a table with an alarm clock
on it. The clock reads 7.29am.

> WILLIAM
> Dixie Dean was the greatest
> centre forward of all time.
> Least that's what my grandad
> says. He played football in
> the nineteen twenties, which
> is like a billion years ago.
> But he scored sixty goals in
> thirty-nine games. Sixty! That's
> loads. Nobody's ever been able
> to score that many since.

The clock by the bed flicks on to 7.30am
and the alarm goes off. William reaches
over and, without looking, hits it off.

> WILLIAM (cont.)
> His real name was William.
> William 'Dixie' Dean. That's
> my name, too. William. I think
> it's a sign. I think it's a sign
> that I'm going to be a famous
> football player like Dixie
> one day.

Off screen we hear William's MUM shout.

                    MUM
William! Are you up yet? You're
going to be late for school.

                    WILLIAM
There's just a small matter of
the boots. I've been asking
for some Colt Super Stripes for
ages. Everyone's got Colt Super
Stripes at school. I know that
if I had a pair of Colt Super
Stripes, I'd be as good as Dixie
Dean in no time.

                    MUM
William!

                WILLIAM (to Mum)
OK! I'm up!

INT. CAR. DAY.

William and his little sister, SASHA, 8,
are strapped into the back of the car. The
car is a bit of an old rust bucket. Sasha
is singing along to her MP3 player. William
breathes on the glass, draws a face on it
then wipes it off. As the window clears, we
can see out. Outside the car, Mum and DAD,
both late 40s, are arguing. Dad is in his
dressing-gown. Mum is dressed for work.

                WILLIAM (to camera)
(points) This is my little
sister, Sasha. (points to Mum
and Dad) That's Mum and Dad.

                    WILLIAM (cont.)
          And this (points to car) is the
          car-wreck.

Outside we can hear Mum and Dad arguing.

                         MUM
          It won't start … again!

                         DAD
          What do you want me to do?

                         MUM
          We need a new car.

                         DAD
          We need a miracle. You know we
          can't afford a new car.

                    WILLIAM (to camera)
          Mum and dad are always arguing
          about the car-wreck these days.
          Dad says we can't afford a new
          one on account of the *credit
          crunch*, which sounds more like
          a breakfast cereal to me. The
          credit crunch gets blamed for a
          lot these days. Bet they blame
          the fact that they've forgotten
          my birthday on the credit crunch.

Dad opens William's car door.

                         DAD
          Come on, son. Get out and help
          me push.

William sighs and gets out.

                    WILLIAM (to camera)
          When I become a famous footballer
          the first thing I am going to buy
          is a new car for Mum and Dad.

INT. SCHOOL CORRIDOR. DAY.

William is running along a corridor with his
school bag. He passes a teacher, MR CROSBY,
30s, sporty looking.

                    MR CROSBY
          Walk, William Sparks. Don't run.
          Walk.

                    WILLIAM
          Sorry, sir.

William slows to a hurried walk.

INT. SCHOOL CLASSROOM. DAY.

William enters the classroom where his
teacher, MRS BORKOWSKI, 50s, is taking the
register. The class is full.

                    MRS BORKOWSKI
          Ah, William. Late again!

                    WILLIAM
          Sorry, Mrs Borkowski. The
          car-wreck … I mean, the car
          wouldn't start.

                    MRS BORKOWSKI (sighs)
          Sit down, William.

William looks around for his friends, AJAY and MAI, who are sitting together. He smiles at them. There is no space next to them. He has to sit down next to another boy, KEVIN LEACH, who immediately thumps William on the arm.

                    KEVIN
          You've got a rubbish car! I saw
          you pushing it today (laughs).
          My dad's just got a brand new
          Toyota.

William turns away and looks out the window.

EXT. SCHOOL FIELD. DAY.

William is standing with a big group of other children (mix of boys and girls) from the class including Ajay, Mai and Kevin. They are in their games kits. All of the children have proper football boots on except William who is in his battered old trainers. Mr Crosby is standing in front of the children.

                    MR CROSBY
          Right, listen up. We have some
          big games coming up this term,
          so we need a strong team if we
          are going to stand a chance of
          coming top of the league. I'll
          be picking the team at the end
          of the week. Right now, I'll
          pick two captains who can choose
          their own teams.

Kevin turns and looks at William's feet
then laughs.

> KEVIN
> Can't you afford new boots?
> Rubbish car. Rubbish trainers
> (laughs again).

> WILLIAM (to himself)
> Please don't make Kevin a
> captain. Please don't make
> Kevin a captain.

> MR CROSBY
> Kevin, Mai, out the front.

William sighs. Mai and Kevin go and stand
by Mr Crosby.

> MR CROSBY (cont.)
> Choose your teams.

> WILLIAM (to camera)
> At least Mai will pick me. We've
> been friends for ages.

> Mai
> Sam.

A boy, SAM, steps forward.

> KEVIN
> Ali.

ALI joins Kevin.

> Mai
> Rick.

Another boy, RICK, steps forward.

Slowly, the people disappear around
William. Finally there are two people left.
William, who is looking hurt and cross, and
ANOTHER BOY who is completely uninterested
in what is going on and reading a magazine.
Finally Mai picks William. The teams
separate and put on the different coloured
bibs that Mr Crosby is handing out. They
walk out on to the pitch. Mai is next to
William.

> WILLIAM
> Thanks for picking me last! I
> thought we were friends?

> MAI
> It has nothing to do with
> friendship, Will. This has to do
> with winning. I had to choose
> the best people if we are going
> to beat Kevin's side.

> WILLIAM
> I still can't believe you left
> me until last. You even picked
> Ajay over me. And he has asthma!

> MAI
> He still scored more goals than
> you in the last match we played.
> Will you go in goal?

> WILLIAM
> Oh great! Do I have to?

                    MAI
        Please, Will.

William stomps over to the goal.

            WILLIAM (to camera)
        I bet Dixie Dean never had to
        suffer the humiliation of being
        picked last.

Mr Crosby blows a whistle and the game
starts. William is in goal. We see him miss
several shots as he dives out of the way.
He keeps slipping over in the mud in his
trainers. He quickly gets covered in dirt.
Finally, Kevin takes a shot. William closes
his eyes at the last minute and Kevin kicks
the ball hard at William. It hits William
square in the chest and he falls backwards
in the mud with a groan. He doesn't get up.
Mai and his team run over, looking worried.

INT. HOUSE. DAY.

William walks in through his front door.

                    WILLIAM
          I'm home! Hello? Mum?

There is no answer, so William goes into
the lounge. Mum, Dad, Sasha, William's
GRANDAD, and the family dog, SCRAPHEAP,
are in the lounge. They are wearing party
hats. On the table there are some presents
laid out and a big chocolate cake with 11
candles in. Sasha blows a party blower.

               All (except William)
          Surprise!

The dog starts barking.

                    DAD
          Happy birthday, son.

                    MUM
          Bet you thought we'd forgotten
          didn't you?

                    WILLIAM
          Err, well ….

                    GRANDAD
          As if we'd forget your birthday!

                    WILLIAM
          Hello, Grandad.

                    SASHA
          Presents! Open mine.

William opens a box and sees some chocolate cornflake cakes in there.

> SASHA (cont.)
> I made them myself. And the card. I made that too.

Sasha hands William a card with 'Happy Bathday' written on it and a hand drawn picture of William in the bath.

> WILLIAM
> Thanks, Sash.

> MUM
> This one's from us.

> WILLIAM (to camera)
> Please make it be a pair of Colt Super Stripes. Please!

William opens a box and sees some football socks and a book about Dixie Dean. He tries not to let his disappointment show.

> WILLIAM
> Thanks, Mum, Dad.

> MUM
> I know it wasn't quite what you wanted, but, well …

> WILLIAM
> No, they're great. Really.

Dad takes off his party hat.

                    DAD
Sorry, son. I have to go
to work.

                  GRANDAD
But I haven't given him my
present yet!

                    DAD
You don't need me here for that.
I'm going to be late at this
rate. I can't afford to be late
for work. You understand, don't
you, Will?

             WILLIAM (sadly)
Course, Dad. I know you have
to go.

                    DAD
Sorry, son.

Dad gives William a quick hug then leaves
the room.

                    MUM
I'll fix your tea. Lasagne OK?

                  WILLIAM
Great.

Mum also leaves the room. Sasha is bored
and puts on the TV.

                  GRANDAD
Here you go, William.

Grandad hands William a shoebox-shaped present.

> WILLIAM
> What's this?

> GRANDAD
> Open it, you daft donkey!

> WILLIAM (to camera)
> Oh please, oh please!

William rips the paper off and opens the box. Inside are a pair of old, brown leather football boots with studs on the bottom. They look worn and well used. They are certainly not the new pair of Colt Super Stripes he wanted.

> GRANDAD
> Well?

Again, William tries to hide his disappointment. He takes a sip of drink from a cup on the table.

> WILLIAM
> Err … thanks, Grandad.

> GRANDAD
> I got them in a second hand shop, on the High Street.

> WILLIAM (to camera)
> I can't wear these at school. I'll be laughed at!

GRANDAD

The bloke who sold them swore
they were worn by Dixie Dean
himself.

WILLIAM

No way!

GRANDAD

On my life, he swore Dixie
wore these very boots when
he was a kid.

WILLIAM (to camera)

Well, they certainly look old
enough to have come from the
last century. Of course I don't
believe him. But I know it will
make Grandad happy if he thinks
I do.

GRANDAD

Try them on then.

WILLIAM

Err … OK.

William puts the boots on the floor. The
dog comes up and sniffs them, growls,
then whimpers and runs away.

GRANDAD

Stupid dog.

William tries the boots on. He wiggles his
toes, then lifts one foot then the other.

                    WILLIAM (to camera)
        The funny thing is, when I try
        them on for the first time, I get
        a strange tingling sensation all
        the way up my legs. And I'm sure
        it's not pins and needles.

                        GRANDAD
        Well?

Grandad is smiling.

                        WILLIAM
        They feel … good! I want to try
        them out. (calls out of the room
        to the kitchen) Mum, I'm going to
        the park! I mean, if that's OK?

                    MUM (off screen)
        Just for an hour then. And take
        the dog!

EXT. PARK. DAY.

William is in the middle of an empty
football pitch, on the centre line. He is
in his football kit and his new/old boots.
He is holding a football. The dog is sitting
watching him. William puts the ball on the
ground. He prepares himself to kick the
ball, aiming at the goal. He kicks the ball
and gets it in the back of the net. It is a
great shot. William looks from the goal to
his feet to the dog.

WILLIAM
Blimey, Scrapheap. Come on!

William runs after the ball. The dog barks
and runs after him. We see William take
several more shots, each from a different
angle, each one tricky. Every time they go
in the net.

INT. HOUSE. DAY.

In the lounge Mum, Grandad and Sasha are
sitting down to tea. The front door bangs
and William walks into the room. He is
covered in mud.

MUM
William! You're covered!

GRANDAD
How were the boots?

William smiles at Grandad.

WILLIAM
Fantastic!

Scrapheap enters, looking exhausted from
all the running around, and flops on to
the carpet.

MUM
Never mind the boots … you've
killed the dog!

Sasha starts laughing.

EXT. SCHOOL FIELD. DAY.

William is standing with Ajay, Mai and the
others trying out for the football team.
He's wearing his old/new boots. The players
have already been split into two teams –
the same as in the previous match. Both
teams are standing a little way apart from
each other, talking tactics. Mr Crosby is
talking to Kevin's team.

                    MAI
          Right. I'll play centre forward
          with Sam as before. Rick, you're
          centre midfield with Ajay on
          your left.

Ajay takes a puff on his inhaler.

                    AJAY
          OK.

                    MAI
          William, you're left back.

                    WILLIAM
          Can't I play up front? Please!

Mai winces.

                    MAI
          No. I can't risk it!

                    WILLIAM
          But I've been practising really
          hard.

                    MAI
        No one can improve that much in
        a week.

                    AJAY
        Come on, Mai. Give him a break.
        You know Kevin had it in for him
        last time.

They look over at Kevin's team who have
moved to take their positions on the pitch.
Kevin comes close to Mai's team.

                    MAI
        Sorry, Will.

                  WILLIAM
        But I've got new boots!

Mai looks at William's feet. Kevin, who has
overheard their conversation, also looks at
William's feet.

                   KEVIN
        Ha! Call them new boots, Sparks?
        Look at them! They look like
        they were made from bits of road
        kill. Loser!

                  WILLIAM
        These boots were once worn by
        Dixie Dean!

                   KEVIN
        Who? Trust you to have
        second-hand boots. They're naff.

                    AJAY
          Shut up, Kevin.

Kevin squares up to them.

                    KEVIN
          Yeah? What are you going to do
          about it, puffa boy?

                    MAI
          Ignore him.

                    MR CROSBY
          Come on you lot!

They take their positions. The game begins.
William plays brilliantly. We see him tackle
several members of Kevin's team, helping to
stop several goals; he even tackles the ball
from Kevin, passing it to a mid-fielder who
scores. Mai gives William a big smile. Then
Ajay takes a puff on his inhaler. He has to
stop. Mr Crosby blows the whistle and goes
over to Ajay. William and Mai also run over.

                    MR CROSBY
          You OK, Ajay?

                    AJAY
          Think I just need to sit
          down, sir.

                    MR CROSBY
          OK.

                    MAI
          But that will leave us
          one player down!

MR CROSBY
There's not much I can do about
that. Why don't you move
William up?

Ajay leaves the pitch and gives William a wink
on the way. William smiles at him. The game
resumes. William quickly gains possession
of the ball and scores a fantastic goal. The
other team are totally shocked. They play
on. Kevin gets the ball. William tackles
him, passes to Rick, who passes back. William
scores again. Mai's side win the game.

INT. CHANGING ROOM. DAY.

William and Ajay have got changed back into
their school uniforms. William is tying
his shoelaces. Ajay is packing his bag.

AJAY
You were amazing, Will! Two goals!
Did you see Kevin's face!

WILLIAM
It's not me. It's my new boots!

AJAY
What do you mean? Of course it's
you!

WILLIAM
I'm telling you, it's the boots.
Ever since I put them on, I've
just been able to play really
well. They must be miracle boots
or something.

                    AJAY
        Yeah right!

                    WILLIAM
        Serious! I mean you know how
        badly I played before.

                    AJAY
        Yeah, but *miracle boots!*
        Honestly, Will.

                    WILLIAM
        Well they did belong to
        Dixie Dean!

                    AJAY
        Oh, come on!

Ajay starts laughing and slaps William on
the back in a friendly way. We see William
put his boots in his bag. They stand up and
walk over to the door of the changing rooms.
As they get up to leave, we see Kevin hiding
behind a locker. He has been listening to
their conversation.

                    WILLIAM
        Thanks, by the way.

                    AJAY
        What for?

                    WILLIAM
        For pretending to be sick.

                    AJAY
        I have no idea what you're
        talking about!

William and Ajay leave, grinning to each other. Kevin narrows his eyes and smiles.

INT. HOUSE. DAY.

William runs into the lounge. Grandad and Sasha are playing a board game. Scrapheap is lying on the carpet. William dumps his bag down. He looks breathless and happy.

>   WILLIAM
>   I'm in the team! Grandad, I'm
>   in the team! Midfield as well!
>   First game's tomorrow!

Grandad looks very happy. Sasha just rolls her eyes.

>   GRANDAD
>   That's great, William.
>   Just great!

>   WILLIAM
>   It's the boots, Grandad!

>   GRANDAD
>   Didn't I tell you?

>   SASHA
>   Does this mean I have to come and
>   stand in the cold and watch you?

>   GRANDAD
>   It certainly does! We'll all be
>   there.

Mum enters wearing an apron and carrying some cakes.

                    MUM
          Where will we all be?

                    GRANDAD
          Ah, cake. Perfect timing. We're
          celebrating. Our William's just
          got in the football team.

                    MUM
          That's fantastic news!
          Well done!

INT. BEDROOM. DAY.

William is lying in bed. He is reading his
Dixie Dean book. The clock reads 7.29am.

                    WILLIAM (to camera)
          Dixie Dean was amazing. Scored
          379 goals in 438 games. He was
          never booked or sent off once.
          Not like Kevin Leach yesterday.
          He was sent off for tackling Sam
          from behind. Sam fell over and
          hurt his knee which has meant
          that he can't play today. I
          think Kevin knows that Sam is
          better than him and didn't want
          him to play centre forward.

The alarm clock goes off. William glances
at it and turns it off.

                    WILLIAM (to camera)
          It's OK. It's Saturday. Game's
          not till eleven.

Sasha comes bursting in through the door.

                    WILLIAM
          Come in why don't you!

                    SASHA
          Mum says, have you got your
          smelly old football kit ready
          for today?

                    WILLIAM
          My kit! I forgot to put it in
          the wash!

William jumps out of bed. He rushes over to
his bag and opens it. He pulls his kit out.

                    WILLIAM
          My boots! They're not here!

William frantically searches his bag, then
his room.

                    WILLIAM (cont.)
             Where are they? Mum! *Mum!*

Mum comes in to the room and picks up his
kit from the floor.

                    MUM
          What is it? Anyone would think
          you were lost at sea the way
          you're shouting and hollering.
          Look at the state of these! Why
          didn't you put them in the wash
          last night? If I put them in
          now, they may just dry.

                    WILLIAM
          It's my boots! They're gone.

                      MUM
          What do you mean gone? How can
          they be gone?

                    WILLIAM
          They're not here!

                      MUM
          You probably left them at
          school.

                    WILLIAM
          No, I remember putting them in
          my bag last night.

William, Mum, Sasha and Scrapheap run
around the house looking for the boots.
William looks very upset.

                      MUM
            Sorry, son. You'll just have to
            play in your trainers.

                    WILLIAM
            I can't! You don't understand.
            They were Dixie Dean's boots!
            They were miracle boots!

                      MUM
            Dixie Dean? Miracle boots! They
            were your grandad's when he was
            a boy. Dixie Dean's indeed. Who
            told you that?

                    WILLIAM (quietly)
          Grandad.

Mum looks sympathetically at William.

INT. CHANGING ROOM. DAY.

William has changed into his football
shorts.

                    WILLIAM (to camera)
          Dixie Dean had a motorbike
          accident in 1926. He fractured
          his skull and jaw. The doctors
          said he would never play
          football again. The next year
          he broke the world record for
          scoring the most goals in one
          season. He didn't give up. I'm
          not going to give up either.

Ajay comes round the corner as William is
pulling on his football shirt. William
makes a 'yuck' face. Ajay is already
dressed in his kit.

                    AJAY
          What's up?

                    WILLIAM
          My shirt is still damp! Mum
          had to wash it this morning.

Ajay takes out his inhaler and takes a puff
on it. William pulls out his trainers from
his bag. Ajay looks at him in alarm.

                    AJAY
        Where are your miracle boots?

William looks miserable.

                    WILLIAM
        I don't know! I could've swore
        I put them in my bag yesterday
        lunchtime. Anyway, I thought
        you didn't believe in the
        miracle boots?

                    AJAY
        Yeah, but that's before I knew we
        were playing Grimswell Juniors! We
        need all the miracles we can get.

Mr Crosby comes round the corner.

                    MR CROSBY
        Come on, boys. I need the team
        out front for a quick chat.

EXT. SCHOOL FIELD. DAY.

Mr Crosby's team are all gathered round.
The team includes, amongst others, William,
Mai, Ajay, Kevin, Rick and Ali. Kevin
is standing well away from William and
does not look at him. There are lots of
spectators gathered round the edge of the
pitch including Grandad, Mum and Sasha.

                    MR CROSBY
        Right, slight change of plan.
        William you are going to play
        centre forward alongside Kevin.

> WILLIAM
> Me? What? What about Mai?

> MR CROSBY
> You and Mai are swapping places.

> WILLIAM
> But I really don't think …

William looks at Mai.

> MAI
> I asked to be swapped.

> WILLIAM
> Why?

> MAI
> This isn't about friendship,
> Will. This is about winning!

Mai gives William a broad smile.

> MR CROSBY
> Grimswell are a tough side. They
> are going to be hard to beat.
> But just work together, keep it
> tight, and you will win.

William and the others walk out on to the
pitch. As they do so, William notices that
Kevin is walking a little awkwardly. He is
wearing William's boots.

> WILLIAM
> Hey! You've got my boots on!

Kevin faces him angrily.

                    KEVIN
          Mine were a bit dirty. I didn't
          think you'd mind if I borrowed
          yours.

                    WILLIAM
          You stole them from my bag!

                    KEVIN
          Borrowed.

                    WILLIAM
          Take them off, now!

                    KEVIN
          Make me, loser!

Just then the whistle blows and the game
begins. Mai kicks the ball. It comes sailing
towards William, who misses it because he is
still looking angrily at Kevin. He realizes
what has happened and chases after the ball.
William plays well. He makes some nice passes
and opens up some chances for other players,
but the pitch is slippery and he keeps
sliding everywhere because his trainers have
no studs on. He misses the ball and the other
team score. As the game goes on, William and
his team fall behind. Kevin begins to look
more and more uncomfortable running up and
down. At one point there is a clear run at
the goal. William has the ball but he is
being marked heavily.

                    WILLIAM
          Kevin!

William passes the ball to Kevin. Kevin misses a really easy goal. At half time, they are two nil down. William's team leave the pitch looking miserable. Kevin limps awkwardly off.

INT. CHANGING ROOM. DAY.

Mr Crosby's team are all gathered together in the changing room. Kevin takes William's boots off and throws them at William.

> KEVIN
> Here, have your crummy
> boots back!

Kevin pulls his socks off to reveal some really nasty blisters.

> MR CROSBY
> What on earth has happened to
> you, Kevin?

> KEVIN
> My boots rubbed.

> WILLIAM (quietly to Ajay)
> *My* boots you mean!

William and Ajay try not to laugh as William puts on his old boots.

> MR CROSBY
> Well you can't play like that.

> KEVIN
> But, sir! I'm fine.

Kevin tries to stand up, but winces and has to sit back down again.

> MR CROSBY
> No. You're out. We'll bring on Jamal. As for the rest of you, what is going on out there? You're playing as if you've never played before. I'm changing the formation. We need a strong defence so we're going for the four-five-one. That's four defenders and five midfielders, and that leaves you, William, as our only striker.

There is a bit of muttering from the team.

> MR CROSBY (cont.)
> You are only two down. You can still win this.

EXT. SCHOOL FIELD. DAY.

The teams run back out on to the pitch. William looks over at his family and sees that his dad has joined them. Dad gives him a huge grin.

> MAI
> Good luck, William. I know you can do it!

The game resumes. William has a new lease of life now he can keep upright in his boots. William and the others

play brilliantly. The other team start
to fall behind. William scores one goal,
then another. It is a tense game. But
in the last two minutes William scores a
hat-trick. He wins the game for his team.
Everyone cheers and runs up to him apart
from Kevin who is looking miserable and
sitting on the side lines with his feet
soaking in a bowl of water.

EXT. CAR PARK. DAY.

William is still in his football kit but
has his coat on and has his bag with him.
He says goodbye to Mai and Ajay then runs
over to the car-wreck where Mum, Dad,
Sasha, Grandad and the dog (on lead) are
waiting. Dad gives him a hug. The dog
growls and barks at William's boots.

> DAD
> Sorry I was late, son.

> WILLIAM
> That's OK. I'm just glad you
> made it.

> DAD
> I took the afternoon off. I
> wasn't going to miss your first
> big game now was I.

> MUM
> This calls for a celebration.
> Come on, get in. I'm taking us
> out … my treat.

Dad puts the dog in the boot (it has dog bars to separate it from the passengers). Mum climbs in the passenger door. William, Grandad and Sasha get in the back – William is in the middle. They put their seat belts on. William and Grandad speak quietly to each other.

> GRANDAD
> So, how are the boots?

> WILLIAM
> They are miracle boots!

> GRANDAD
> I told you!

> WILLIAM
> It's funny though, because Mum says they were your boots when you were my age.

> GRANDAD
> Ah, yes, so they were.

> WILLIAM
> But you said they belonged to Dixie Dean! You said the bloke in the shop who sold them to you told you that.

> GRANDAD
> Well, that's what he told me … when I bought them. I didn't say I bought them last week, did I? I bought them when I was a lad. Did wonders for my game! They really are miracle boots.

Dad gets in the driver's door.

> WILLIAM
> So you still really think they
> belonged to Dixie Dean?

> GRANDAD
> What do you think?

Dad turns the key in the ignition. It
doesn't start.

> MUM
> Not again!

Dad turns round to William.

> DAD
> Come on, son. Get out and help
> me push.

William sighs and gets out.

> WILLIAM (to camera)
> Yes, when I become a famous
> footballer the very first thing
> I am going to buy is a new car.

End music/credits.

> THE END

At Night

By Alex Lane
Illustrated by Paul McCaffrey

At night, my imagination
follows me up the stairs,
I can feel it in the shadows
prickling my arm hairs.
I can feel it shiver up my back,
and whisper in the air,
telling me it's hungry,
hungry for nightmares.

At night, my imagination
knocks on my bedroom door,
if I don't get up and let it in,
it stalks across the floor.
It rattles at the handle
and scratches with its claws,
and I know that it is hungry,
hungry like before.

At night, my imagination keeps me up late at night,
reading in my tent of covers, eyes heavy from torchlight.
It waits until I'm asleep
and my eyelids are shut tight,
then it licks its lips, still hungry,
hungry for a bite.

At night, my imagination
can be covered in slime and scales,
or sometimes it can be made of
metal held with screws and nails.
Sometimes it has a pelt of fur
or a back of thick black hair,
but all the time it's hungry,
hungry for nightmares.

At night, my imagination
scuttles from under my bed,
it grabs me with its hairy legs
and spins me in a web.
I wake up twisted in blankets,
hot and drenched in sweat,
then I know my imagination
is hungry but well fed.

Find out more ...

For more **unexplained** stories read,

Storm Chasers ...

and Tasmanian Terror.